Mallard Duck at Meadow View Pond

For Andrew, Tim, Jaime, and all children who like to feed mallard ducks — W.P.

To Pooh — T.O.

Book layout: Marcin D. Pilchowski
Editor: Judy Gitenstein
Editorial assistance: Chelsea Shriver

First Edition 2001
10 9 8 7 6 5 4 3 2
Printed in China

Acknowledgments:
   Our very special thanks to Dr. Gary R. Graves of the Department of Vertebrate Zoology at the Smithsonian Institution's National Museum of Natural History for his curatorial review.

Mallard Duck at Meadow View Pond

by Wendy Pfeffer
Illustrated by Taylor Oughton

4

Near the yard of the farmhouse at Meadow View Pond, over the fence and down the gentle slope where meadow and water meet, a mallard hen sits on her nest. Her earth-colored feathers hide her in the brush and grasses from the crows and raccoons that eat eggs.

Inside the eight creamy tan eggs that the mallard hen has warmed and guarded for four weeks, there is now sound and movement. Only she hears the duckling chipping his way out of his smooth porcelain shell. Far out where the spring sun shines through the mist on the old farm pond, her mate's iridescent green head glistens among those of the other drakes.

Seven more ducklings hatch during the day.
Each uses its egg-tooth like a little hammer
to peck its way out of its smooth, hard shell.
By day's end, exhausted by their effort,
five male and three female ducklings
huddle under their mother,
peeping sleepily.

The next day, the firstborn mallard and his seven siblings waddle behind their mother as she leads them to the warm, shallow water of the pond. The ducklings do not need swimming lessons. They paddle right off behind their mother while she checks her brood for stragglers.

Their brown-and-yellow down makes the ducklings look like yellow pond lilies. While the ducklings were hatching, insect eggs were also hatching, making enough food for the ducklings to eat. Mallard Duck skims a mayfly from the water and picks water fleas off a plant stem. He stabs the water with his bill and catches a water bug.

A nearby hawk sees food. It circles and swoops down toward the ducklings. The mother duck stretches her neck and sees the danger. Quickly she hides her brood in the weeds and reeds along the shore. She moves away, flapping her wings, splashing water, and quacking loudly. She rises up, then drops to the water again and again, one wing bent at an angle to look like it is broken. This commotion distracts the hawk from its prey. It gives up its chase and flies away.

The brood is safe from the hawk, but a greater danger lurks as the ducklings come out of their hiding place. A snapping turtle has been watching and waiting under water, partly hidden in the mud. Now it snaps at the last duckling in line. The little ducks scatter out of the turtle's reach as the mother hurries her brood to land. They are all safe for now. Next time, one or two ducklings may not be so lucky.

On shore, the mother duck nestles her young while she watches for foxes or skunks ready to spring out of the tall grass. A chilly rain begins to fall. The mother duck spreads her wings to keep her ducklings dry and warm.

Most days are warm and sunny. The mother duck leads her young out on the pond. The ducklings bob like corks, then glide over the water without appearing to move at all, but under the water, their feet are paddling furiously.

The mother duck tips her tail straight up and her neck straight down to reach snails, fish eggs and plants below the surface of the water. Mallard Duck pulls plants out by the roots and nibbles on them. His bill is perfect for eating underwater plants. It acts as a sieve, trapping food while letting the water drain out.

In the middle of the day Mallard Duck naps, nestled close to his siblings, while their mother preens her feathers. Mallard Duck soaks up the warm rays of the June sun. He is now five weeks old and has lost his fluffy yellow down. He and his siblings are covered with soft feathers of brown and gray.

Mallard Duck's oil glands have now begun to work, and he is able to preen himself. First he shakes his whole body, then he uses his beak to smooth his juvenile feathers. While he's smoothing the feathers, his beak passes over the gland at the base of his tail and spreads the oil to keep his feathers waterproof.

23

Soon the mother duck molts and sheds her wing feathers. She will not be able to fly for nearly a month. She hides in the grass and watches her ducklings, unable to protect them. When danger lurks, she dives underwater or swims away.

25

By late summer Mallard Duck and his siblings are almost full-grown. Their flight feathers are ready to be tested. They flap their wings to exercise them. Soon their wings are powerful enough to lift the ducklings up into the air. They practice taking off, flying and landing.

In September Mallard Duck's colorful adult plumage of bright feathers has grown in, and he and his four brothers are now mature mallard drakes, like their father. The three female ducklings are now mature mallard hens, brown like their mother.

On frosty late autumn mornings, the water of Meadow View Pond has begun to freeze. Soon ice will cover the food supply. Mallard Duck will migrate with some of his siblings and other ducks to a southern lake for the winter. There he will find a mate, and in the spring he will follow her to the place where she was hatched. Over the fence of the house at Meadow View Pond and down that same pasture slope, Mallard Duck's mother will again sit on a nest and another clutch of mallard ducklings will hatch.

About the Mallard Duck

The mallard, whose species name is *Anas platyrhynchos*, is the most widely-known duck in the world, and is found almost everywhere in the northern hemisphere, from isolated woodland lakes to ponds in the middle of the largest cities.

The mallard is known as a dabbler and can often be seen with its tail straight up in the air and the rest of its body submerged while it searches for food below the surface of the water.

In spring the male mallard, the drake, shows off his beautiful colors to attract a mate. He nods, splashes, sprays, rears up, and spreads his wings. He and his mate feed, swim, and play together. The drake defends his mate while she chooses a nesting place, usually near water.

A mallard hen lays between seven and twelve eggs. They hatch in the order they were laid. The same day that all the eggs hatch, the mallard hen leads her young to water where they feed themselves.

The hen is a very attentive mother and is fiercely protective of her ducklings. She often lures predators away from her brood by pretending to have a broken wing. When she escapes, she hurries back to her ducklings.

When mallards migrate, they follow flyways. Some may fly three thousand miles, often traveling 60 miles per hour, as fast as a car on a highway.

The mallard is still the most abundant duck in the world, but hunters and pollution are depleting the mallard population. Fortunately, places have been set aside by conservationists where mallards can rest and feed safely. Mallards help people by eating mosquito larvae that grow into disease-carrying mosquitoes. We can help mallards by protecting their wetland habitats.

Glossary

brood: A group of birds hatched at one time and cared for together.
clutch: A nest of eggs.
egg-tooth: A sharp horny growth at the tip of a bird's beak.
flyways: Age-old routes used by all migrating birds.
preen: To smooth and clean the feathers with the bill or beak.
siblings: Brothers and sisters.